To Pen, with love and welcome

—L. S. P.

*This book is for everyone who has supported
my broken crayon art over the years—thank you.
You never know what will come out of a broken crayon!*

—D. R. O.

SIMON & SCHUSTER BOOKS FOR YOUNG READERS
An imprint of Simon & Schuster Children's Publishing Division
1230 Avenue of the Americas, New York, New York 10020
Text copyright © 2020 by Linda Sue Park
Illustrations copyright © 2020 by Debbie Ridpath Ohi
SIMON & SCHUSTER BOOKS FOR YOUNG READERS is a trademark of Simon & Schuster, Inc.
For information about special discounts for bulk purchases, please contact Simon & Schuster Special Sales
at 1-866-506-1949 or business@simonandschuster.com.
The Simon & Schuster Speakers Bureau can bring authors to your live event. For more information or to book an event,
contact the Simon & Schuster Speakers Bureau at 1-866-248-3049 or visit our website at www.simonspeakers.com.
Book design by Laurent Linn
The text for this book was set in Banda Regular.
The illustrations for this book were rendered digitally.
Manufactured in China
0620 SCP
First Edition
2 4 6 8 10 9 7 5 3 1
Library of Congress Cataloging-in-Publication Data
Names: Park, Linda Sue, author. | Ohi, Debbie Ridpath, 1962– illustrator.
Title: Gurple and Preen / Linda Sue Park ; illustrated by Debbie Ridpath Ohi.
Description: First edition. | New York : Simon & Schuster Books for Young Readers, [2020] | Summary:
"When Gurple and Preen crash land onto a strange alien planet, they must work together to build something new
from their mistake in order to save their mission"— Provided by publisher.
Identifiers: LCCN 2018038501 (print) | LCCN 2018043327 (ebook) | ISBN 9781534431416 (hardcover) | ISBN 9781534431423 (eBook)
Subjects: | CYAC: Robots—Fiction. | Creative ability—Fiction. | Interplanetary voyages—Fiction.
Classification: LCC PZ7.P22115 (ebook) | LCC PZ7.P22115 Gur 2019 (print) | DDC [E]—dc23
LC record available at https://lccn.loc.gov/2018038501
LC ebook record available at https://lccn.loc.gov/2018043327

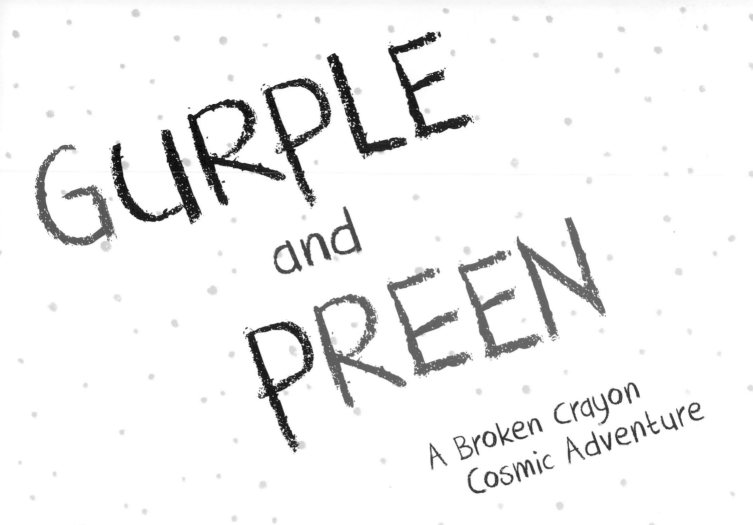

GURPLE and PREEN

A Broken Crayon Cosmic Adventure

Written by
Linda Sue Park

Illustrated by
Debbie Ridpath Ohi

SIMON & SCHUSTER BOOKS FOR YOUNG READERS

NEW YORK LONDON TORONTO SYDNEY NEW DELHI

Gurple's eyes opened, one by one by one.
Her head swiveled as she clanked to her feet.

"Preen?

"PREEN, WHERE ARE YOU?"

The spilled cargo began to shimmy.
Then a bunch of crayons shot into the air.

"Zap my apps!" Gurple yelled, ducking.

Preen launched herself
out from under the pile.

"The pods, the pods!" Gurple waved her arms in a panic. "We're DOOMED without them!"

Preen beeped. She pointed
toward a corner of the pile.

"Oh. **There** they are," Gurple said with a whistle of relief.
"But look at the **rest** of this mess!

"How are we ever going to repair the ship?
It's impossible!
We need solar-powered batteries, fusion
plasma engines, magnetic force fields—"

Gurple picked up a blue crayon and broke it. "Bits and bytes—a *tablecloth*? What are we supposed to do with that? We need stuff we can *use*."

Gurple broke a brown crayon. A flock of quails
fluttered out and began running around her feet.

"Shoo! Shoo!

"Can't you see I'm busy?"
Gurple shouted.

Preen rounded up the quails,
bird by bird by bird.

Meanwhile, Gurple was still breaking crayons.

A skateboard. "No time!"

Strings of lights?
"No clue!!"

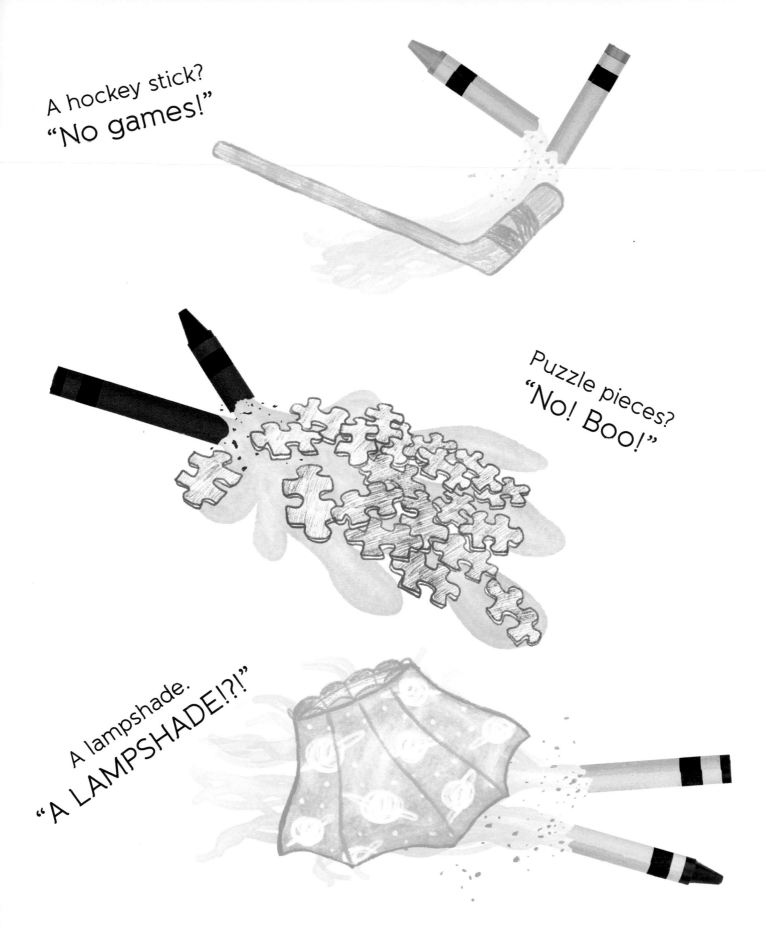

A hockey stick?
"No games!"

Puzzle pieces?
"No! Boo!"

A lampshade.
"A LAMPSHADE!?!"

"We're **never** going to be able to rebuild with nothing but JUNK!" Gurple wailed.

Gurple kept fuming.

Preen kept working, putting
things together bit

by bit

by bit.

Gurple broke a white crayon.

"Itchy glitches!"
she yelled in frustration.

"Robots don't go to the
bathroom!"

Gurple hurried over to check on the pods. "The countdown has started. We'll have to open the pods SOON, and nothing's ready!"

3 HRS 14 MIN...

3 HRS 13 MIN...

3 HRS 12 MIN...

In desperation, she broke another crayon.
A panda jumped out and landed on her head.

"No! Stop!
Quit fooling around!"

Preen beeped.

Gurple looked up in surprise.

"Wow," Gurple said.

"I can't believe it."

Lights on the pods began blinking.

"It's time," Gurple said. Preen beeped again.

They slid the pods out of the box.

"Nodes and codes," Gurple said.
   "Please let this work."

Gurple saluted.
"Commander!"

The commander nodded. "At ease, Gurple.
Have we arrived at our destination?"

"We had to make an emergency landing. The ship
was damaged, but everything has been repaired."

"Good work," the commander said. "How did you do it?"

"Well, it wasn't easy, but—" Gurple stopped.
Her processor whirred and her sensors flashed.
"Um, I mean, Preen did most of it."

"Bip," said Preen. "Bip-bip boop."

"She says they did it the way you do anything hard,"
Gurple translated. "Step by step by step."

Preen beeped. The quails peeped. The panda leaped.

Everyone laughed,
even Gurple.

"Where to next?" Gurple asked.
The commander tapped on her computer.
"Everywhere," she said. "The whole
galaxy. Star by star by star."